FOR BIANCA

Copyright © 1994 by Lena Lenček. All rights reserved. Printed in Hong Kong.

Typeset in Helvetica Condensed. Art Direction by Laura Jane Coats.

Library of Congress Cataloging-in-Publication Data:

Lenček, Lena. The antic alphabet / Lena Lenček.

    p.   cm. ISBN 0-8118-0480-1

1. English language — Alphabet — Juvenile literature.

[1. Alphabet.] I. Title PE1155.L46 1994

[E] — dc20 — dc20 [421'.1] 93-31010 CIP AC

Distributed in Canada by Raincoast Books

112 East Third Avenue, Vancouver, B.C. V5T 1C8

10 9 8 7 6 5 4 3 2 1

Chronicle Books, 275 Fifth Street, San Francisco, California 94103

Thanks to Gideon, Victoria, Molly, Renée & Bibi !!!

THE · ANTIC ALPHABET

LENA LENČEK

Chronicle Books · San Francisco

OLLOW THE ANTIC ALPHABET AS....

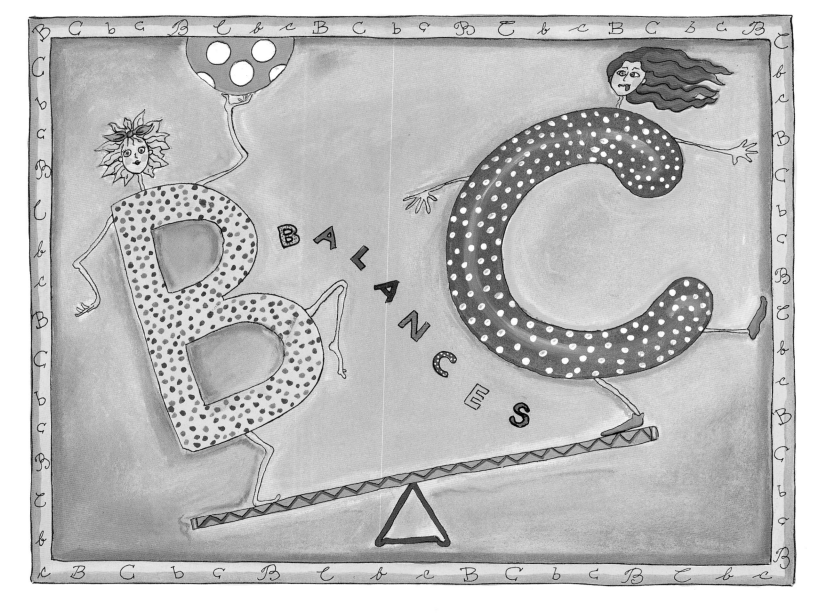

B balances C

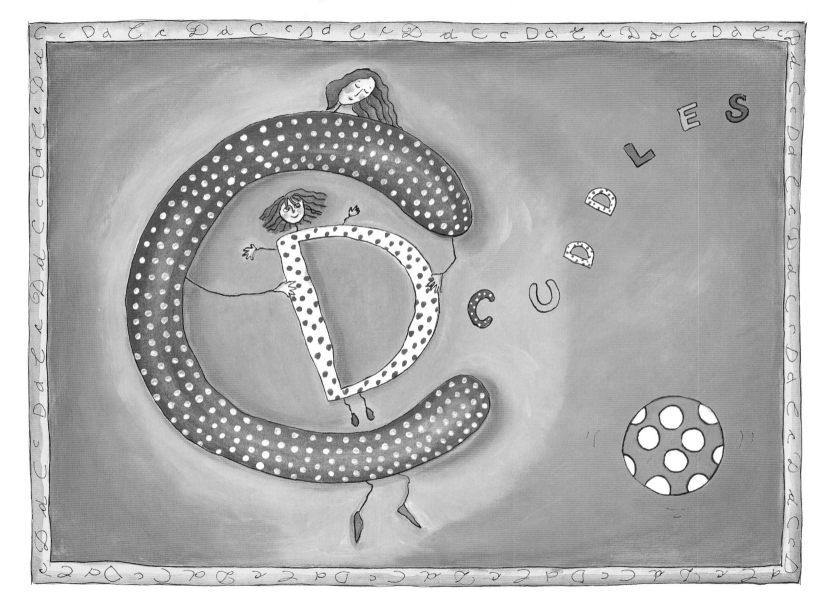

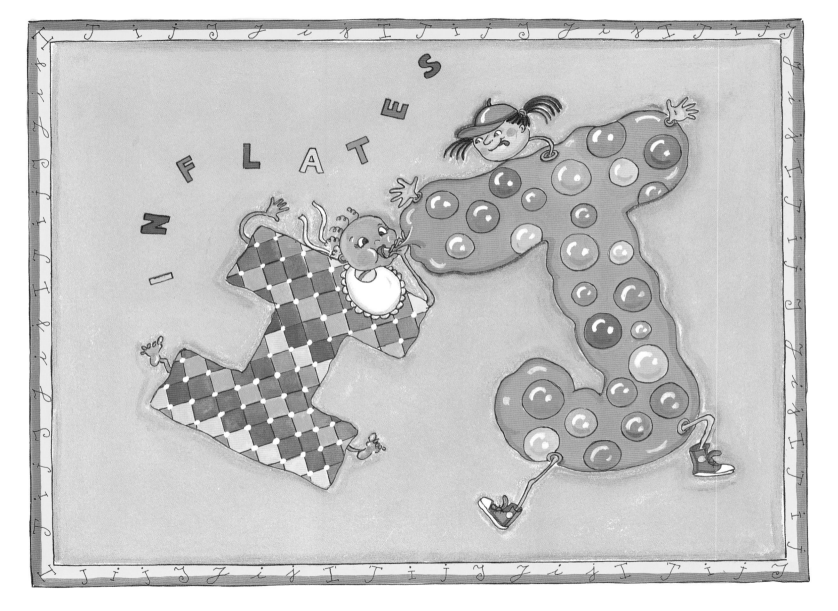

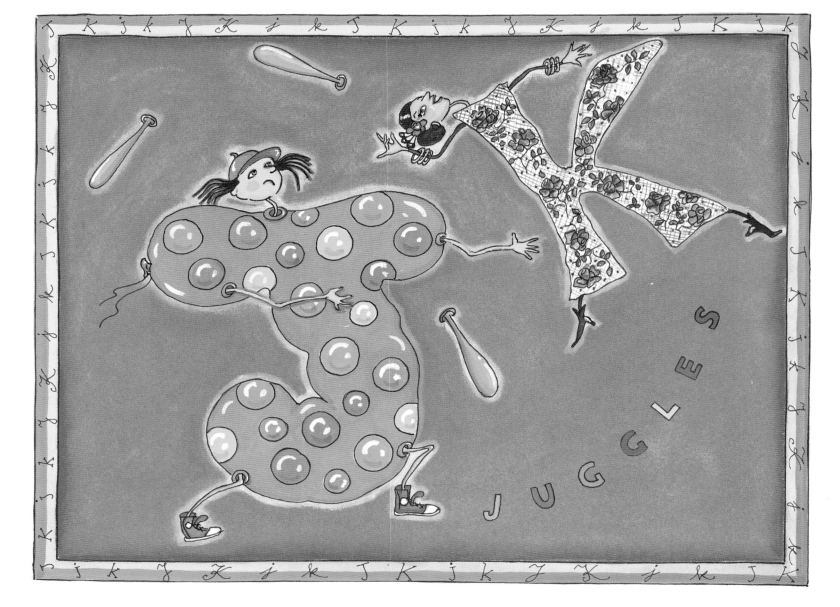

KISSES

LASSOES

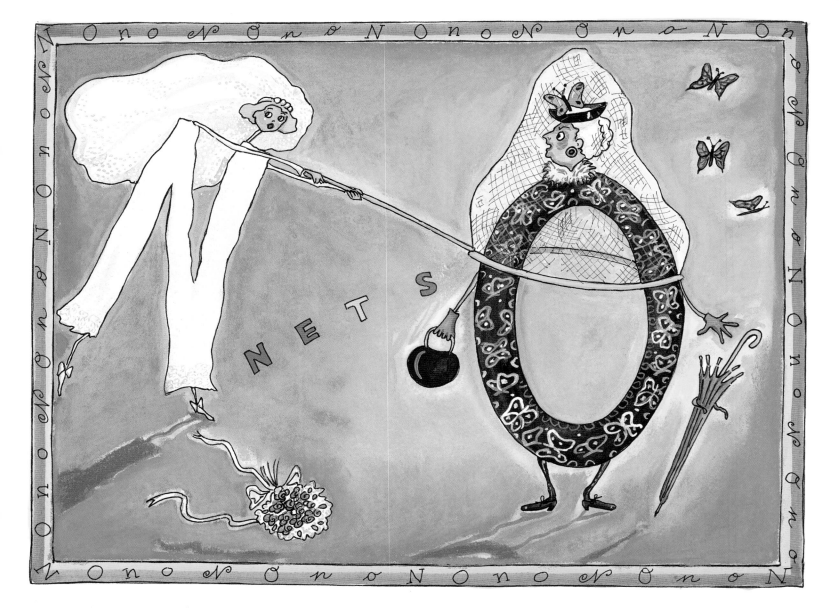

P PUSHES Q

X-RAYS

AND THAT BRINGS US BACK T